E
P Pittar, Gil.
   Milly, Molly and the runaway bean

30000000149074

Milly and Molly

Part of the proceeds from the sale of this book goes to The Friends of Milly, Molly Inc., a charity which aims to promote the acceptance of diversity and the learning of life skills through literacy – *"for every child, a book"*.

Milly, Molly and the Runaway Bean

Published by
MM House Publishing
P O Box 539
Gisborne, New Zealand
email: books@millymolly.com

ISBN: 1-86972-049-0

10   9   8   7   6   5   4   3   2   1

Milly, Molly and the
Runaway Bean

"We may look different
but we feel the same."

Milly and Molly watched Aunt Maude plant her climbing beans. She had one left over.

"Plant this in a sunny place and you will grow fit and healthy on your very own fresh, green beans. And don't forget to water it," she snipped.

Farmer Hegarty gave Milly and Molly a bag of his special sheep manure.
"Feed this to your bean and it too will grow strong and healthy," he said.

Milly and Molly fed and watered their bean
every night.

The bean began to climb.

It climbed up over the wall and into the
lemon tree next door.

It climbed over the fence and into the peach
tree in the garden next door to that.

Milly and Molly ran to find Aunt Maude.
"Our bean won't stop climbing," they said.

Aunt Maude rubbed her chin.
"That bean knows exactly where it's going,"
she snipped. "It will stop when it gets there."

The bean climbed over a potting shed and
through a hedge.

A crowd was beginning to gather. Milly and
Molly's bean was famous.
"Where is it going?" they asked Aunt Maude.

"It knows exactly where it's going," snipped
Aunt Maude. "It will stop when it gets there."

The bean climbed up a drainpipe and in
through a window.

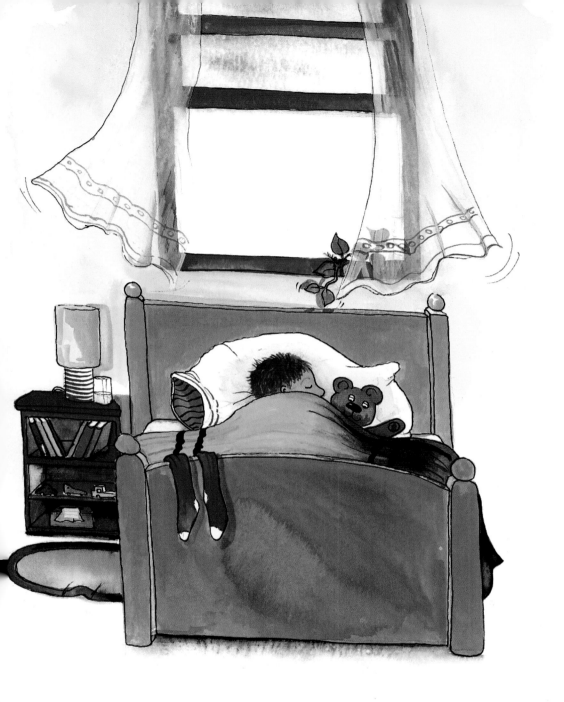

Lying in bed beneath the window was a very
sick little boy.

"I'm going to give you fresh, green beans to make you fit and healthy," whispered the bean.

The sick little boy couldn't believe the
famous bean had come specially to see him.
"Thank you," he said weakly.

The bean stopped climbing. Word got about
that it was giving fresh, green beans to a
little boy who was ill.

"What did I tell you," snipped Aunt Maude. "That bean knew exactly where it was going."

The sick little boy ate the fresh, green beans
and grew stronger and stronger.

Then one morning, he opened his front door and walked out into the sunshine. A mighty cheer went up from the crowd.

"There," snipped Aunt Maude. Our fresh, green beans made you grow fit and healthy."

"I'm sure my bag of special sheep manure had something to do with it," mused Farmer Hegarty.

"Fiddlesticks," snipped Aunt Maude.
"That bean knew exactly where it was
going."

Milly, Molly and the Runaway Bean

The value implicitly expressed in this story is ' good nutrition' - nourishment required by all living things to grow and stay healthy.

Milly and Molly see first-hand how a diet of fresh green beans can contribute to good health. Good nutrition helps make us grow fit and healthy.

"We may look different but we feel the same."